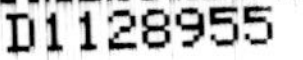

Mama

Vic

Jata

Sophie

Henry

Alexis

duPont

For my granddaughters, Aurora and Chloe, who inspire me every day and for the love of my life, Randy, who is my constant source of joy and encouragement.-I.E.H.

For my myriad nieces and nephews, my models and muses through the years. And for Barks whose constant support, encouragement, and vision got me to the very end. Thank you.-J.L.

Hagley

Illustrations photographed by Mitchell Kearney Photography.
Alexis Irénée du Pont, Frederick D. Henwood, c. 1910-20, Oil on canvas, 92.14.2, Courtesy of Hagley Museum and Library.
Conestoga Powder Wagon, Side View, Photographer Joseph P. Monigle. From "DuPont Company Brandywine Powder Yards and Neighboring Workers Communities Photographs," Acc. 2017.226, Box 9 Folder 5.
Eleuthera du Pont Smith (Mrs. Thomas Mackie Smith), Rembrandt Peale, Philadelphia, Pennsylvania, United States, 1830-31, Oil on canvas, 1967.0277, A Gift of Mr. John Irving Woodriff, Courtesy of Winterthur Museum.
Henry du Pont, Clawson Hammitt, 1919, Oil on canvas, 54.1.490, Courtesy of Hagley Museum and Library.
Letter from Sophie du Pont to Victorine du Pont Bauduy, Feb. 27, 1821. From the Sophie Madeleine Du Pont Papers, Winterthur Manuscripts, Group 9, Item W9-20899.
No. 1 Eleutherian Mills, Charles Dalmas, 1806, Watercolor on paper, 98.24, Courtesy of Hagley Museum and Library.
Profiles of Sophie Madeleine du Pont and Eleuthera du Pont. From the Eleuthera (du Pont) Smith Papers, Winterthur Manuscripts, Group 6, Box 30.
Sophie Madeleine du Pont (Mrs. Samuel Francis Du Pont), Rembrandt Peale, 1831, Oil on canvas, 91.29.2, Courtesy of Hagley Museum and Library.
Sophie Madeleine Dalmas (Mrs. Eleuthère Iréneé du Pont), Joseph Marie Bouton, 1798-99 Watercolor on ivory, 2005.5.1, Courtesy of Hagley Museum and Library.
Victorine du Pont Bauduy (Mme. Ferdinand Bauduy), Rembrandt Peale, New Castle County, Delaware, United States, 1813, Oil on canvas, 1961.0709, A Bequest of Henry Francis du Pont, Courtesy of Winterthur Museum.

Published by Hagley Museum and Library
298 Buck Road
Wilmington, DE 19807
www.hagley.org

Library of Congress Control Number: 2020921754
LC record available at https://lccn.loc.gov/

ISBN 978-0-578-76657-7

Printed in USA
(pb) 10 9 8 7 6 5 4 3 2

The Great Explosion
A Powder Mill Chronicle

Nº 1
ELEUTHERIAN MILLS
1806.
By Chas. Dalmas.

The Great Explosion
A Powder Mill Chronicle

Written by
Ilona E. Holland, Ed.D.

Illustrated by
Judy Love

Despite the warmth of the sun, a chilly draft sent tiny goosebumps up Sophie's neck.

"They shut down the powder mill," Joseph reported.

"Why?" Sophie gasped. She knew the dangers.

Inside, Tata strained to hear what Joseph was telling her younger sister. He did odd jobs for the du Pont family and often brought them news.

"The glazing machine was making strange noises," Joseph continued. "You know how careful they have to be. One spark and the black powder can explode."

“Tata, where are you?” a voice called.

Startled, Tata jumped.
She knew she was supposed to
be getting ready for school. She
turned and raced up the stairs, avoiding
the squeaky steps that would give her away.

Sophie shivered as a whoosh of March air washed over her. “I’m sorry. I have to go. It’s time for lessons.”

She lowered the window, pushing an uneasy feeling down with the sash.

Since grandfather died, the front room on the second floor of the house had been used as a school room. Although Tata, Sophie, and Henry loved to learn, they didn't always enjoy being taught by their oldest sister, Victorine. Vic was strict.

Sometimes Sophie wished she was a boy like Henry. Then Vic would let her study science and languages instead of practicing sewing and cursive writing.

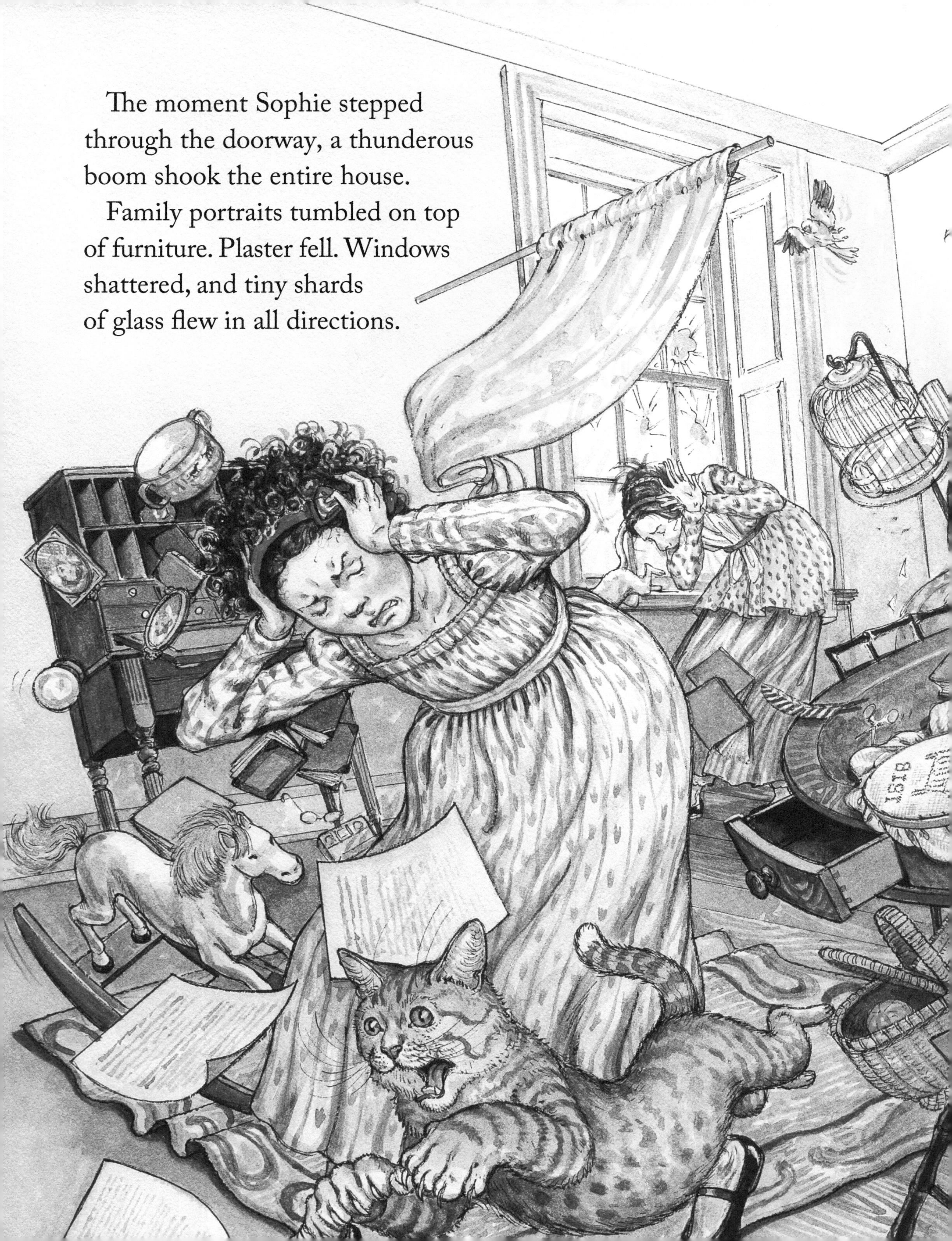

The moment Sophie stepped through the doorway, a thunderous boom shook the entire house.

Family portraits tumbled on top of furniture. Plaster fell. Windows shattered, and tiny shards of glass flew in all directions.

The air smelled strangely burnt and sour. In the distance, a warning bell clanged.

"It's the mill," Sophie yelled. "It's exploding!"

Mama rushed out of her room across the hall. She was clutching the baby. Plaster covered them both.

"*Mes enfants*, hurry! We must get out of the house!"

Mama led the way down the stairs, through the foyer, and out the front door. Then she stopped. Maurice, a trusted workman, stood by the garden gate. Mama handed the baby to him.

"Take Alexis and follow me," she directed. "The powder magazine may blow at any moment! We must get the children to safety. *Mes enfants,* come!"

Together they hurried up the hill between the sweet gum trees. They were well beyond the sand hole when Mama wobbled. No one had noticed that her head was bleeding. She turned unsteadily to check on Maurice and the baby.

She saw to her horror that Maurice, confused and disoriented, was heading back toward the house with Alexis. She knew there could be another explosion at any moment. "Maurice!" she screamed, but her call was swallowed by the distance between them.

Henry clutched Sophie's arm as he watched his mother rush away.

"I'm afraid," he said through tears.

Sophie squeezed her little brother to her. She couldn't let him see that she was scared too. "I'll take care of you," she reassured him.

She closed her eyes and tried to remember what Mama had told her but there was so much noise she couldn't think. Where were they supposed to go?

Suddenly Sophie heard Joseph's familiar voice behind them. "Come with me," he said. "I know a shortcut to the farm. Hurry."

Tata did not notice the three head into the woods. Her eyes were fixed on Mama. Tata held her breath as she watched her mother grab Alexis and climb the hill once more. Halfway up, Mama stopped.

Something was wrong.

Nancy, a house maid, saw her and grabbed the baby just as Mama fainted.

"Mama!" screamed Tata.

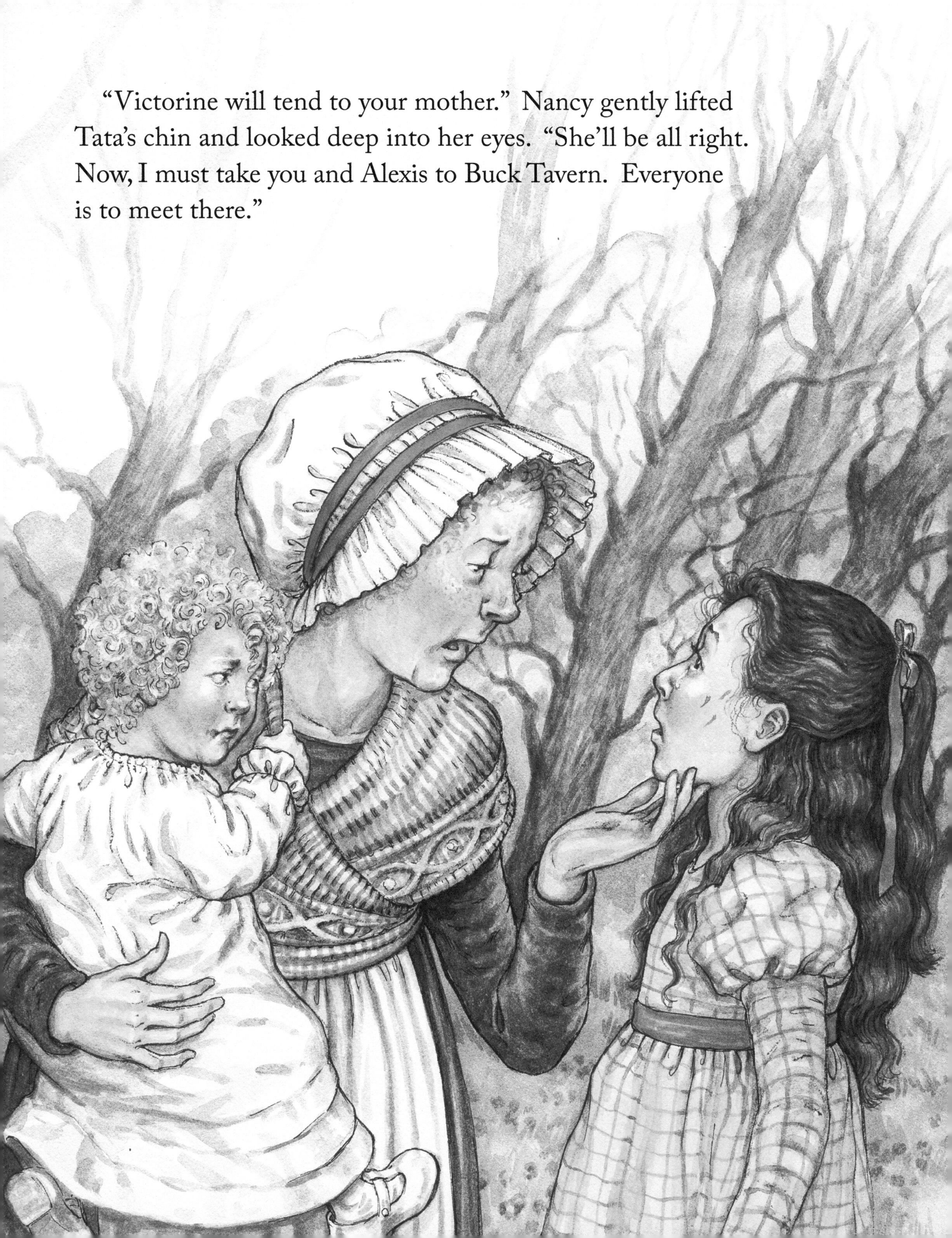

“Victorine will tend to your mother.” Nancy gently lifted Tata’s chin and looked deep into her eyes. “She’ll be all right. Now, I must take you and Alexis to Buck Tavern. Everyone is to meet there.”

At that moment, the worst happened. Flying cinders set the pounding mill aflame. The building exploded and sent sparks onto the granary. The granary exploded next. Rocks, beams, metal and machine parts hurled through the air gouging great holes in the earth wherever they hit.

Finally, the magazine holding thirty-two tons of black powder exploded. Nancy yelled, "***Run!***"

Tata and Nancy ran as fast as they could. The sounds of machinery crashing and tree limbs snapping and the smell of burning timbers urged them forward. They ran without stopping until they reached Buck Tavern almost half a mile away.

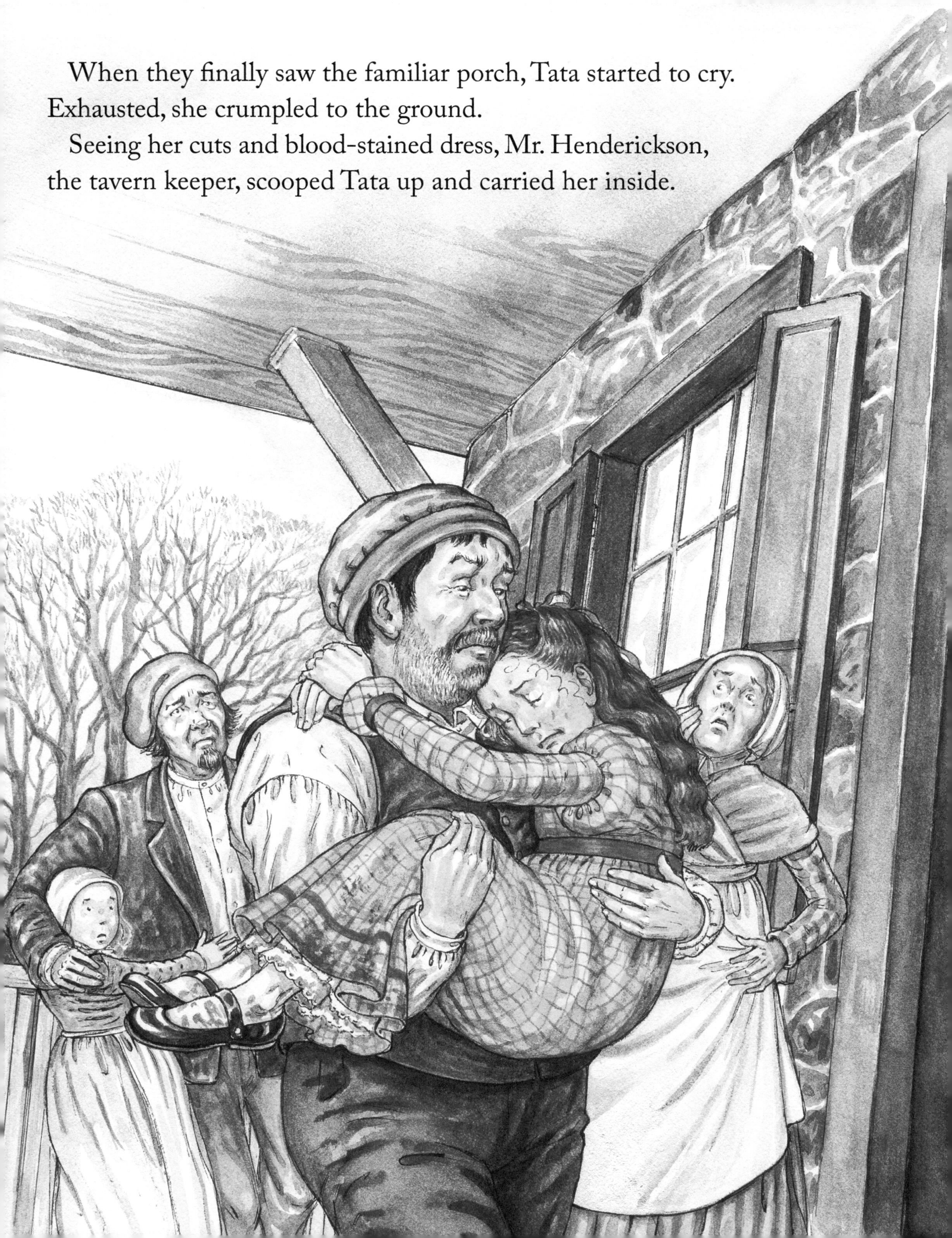

When they finally saw the familiar porch, Tata started to cry. Exhausted, she crumpled to the ground.

Seeing her cuts and blood-stained dress, Mr. Henderickson, the tavern keeper, scooped Tata up and carried her inside.

"Let me take a look at you," he said.
"You are lucky. These cuts are not too deep."

"Please," Tata pleaded. "Put a horse to cart and get Mama. She fainted. Her head is bleeding."

"Don't worry. The men are already out looking for her." Mr. Hendrickson rinsed out the cloth. "Now hold still. I must clean these nicks."

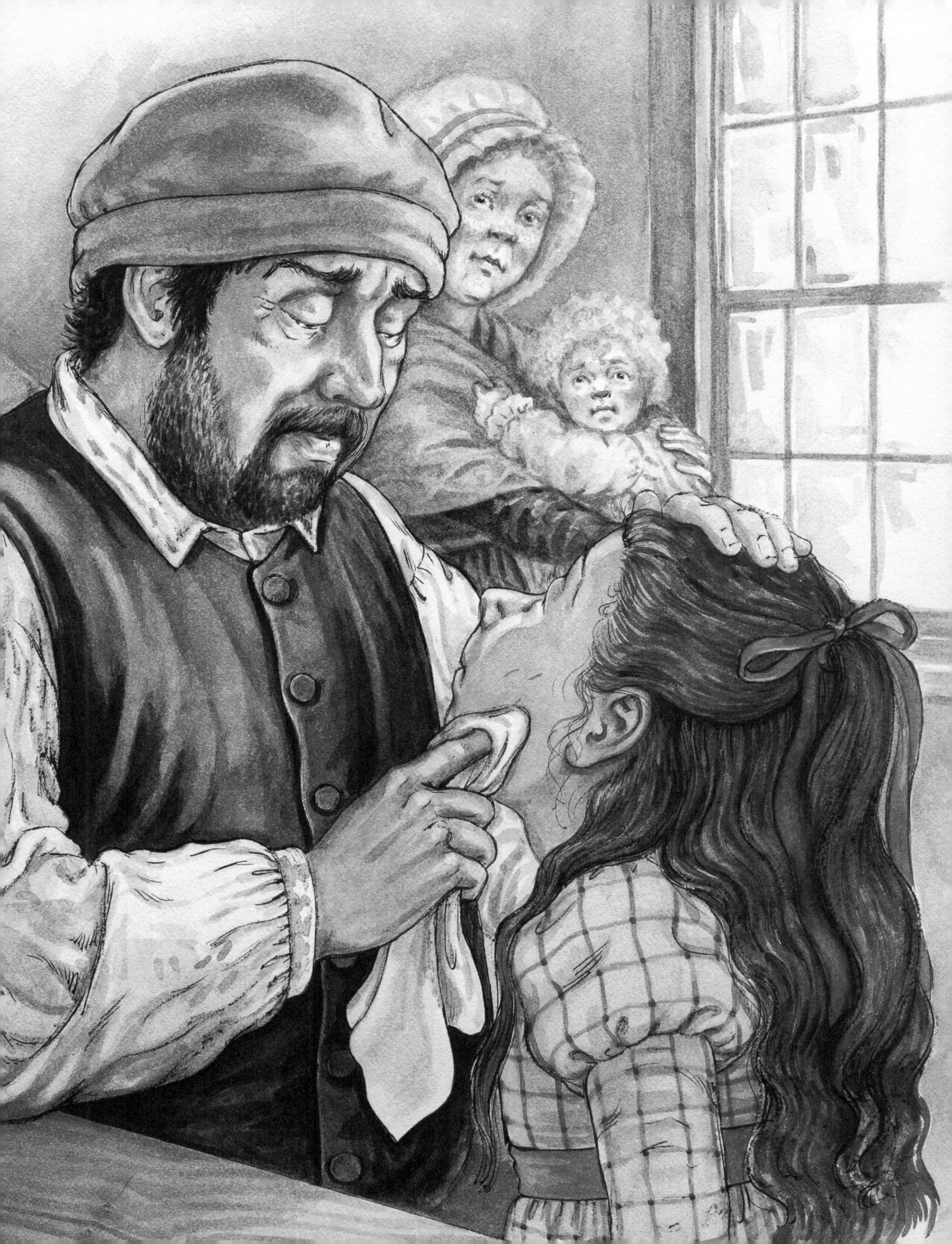

As he finished, the door opened and Mama and Vic walked wearily inside. Tata jumped up, knocking the empty pitcher to the floor.

"Mama!"

“Where are Sophie and Henry?” Mama looked frantically around the room.

Tata and Nancy glanced at each other. “We thought they were with you.”

Mama gasped.

She turned to the men. “Please go and find them! They were not on the road.”

Several of the men called their dogs and began yelling orders. They scattered into the woods and disappeared.

Hours later Tata heard barking. Then the tavern door flew open. Sophie and Henry ran to their mother. “I am sorry, Mama.” Sophie held back tears. “I thought we were to meet at the farm.”

“The rule is to come to the Tavern when you are in danger,” corrected Mama. She pulled the children close. “No matter. We are all together now.”

Tired and hungry, the men assembled around the table. They argued over what had caused the explosion. Many said the foreman had ignored the warnings of the strange machine sounds. Without checking the machinery, he had ordered the mills to restart.

Sophie listened. Her heart ached. Why didn't the foreman check the machinery? Why didn't he do what he knew he was supposed to do?

She had tried to do the right thing, even if she hadn't remembered where she was to meet the others.

Later by the fire Victorine promised that everything would be well again. Papa would be home soon. The mills would be rebuilt and the house repaired.

As Sophie listened, a log shifted sending sparks up the chimney. Sophie's day had shifted too. She had been scared, so scared she thought she might never see her family again. But she also had been brave. At that moment, she knew that she could be brave no matter what. Her heart filled with courage and a small smile flickered across her lips.

Fact from Fiction

The story you read is fiction but it is based on a true historical event. Here are some of the facts that informed the chronicle of *The Great Explosion*.

- **Tata**'s real name was Eleuthera du Pont. Her family called her Tata. She was eleven years old when the explosion occurred and she wrote about it some thirty-five years later. Much of this story was based on her description of what happened.
- **Sophie** (named after her mother) was Tata's younger sister. At the time of the explosion, Sophie was eight, **Henry** was six, and **Alexis** only two.
- **Victorine** was the oldest of the seven children in the family. At twenty-six, she was the teacher for her younger brothers and sisters.
- The family was bilingual, speaking both French and English. **Mama** often spoke to the children in French.
- Parts of the ceiling actually fell on **Mama**'s head. Although she lived, she never fully recovered.
- The children of the workers and the family knew each other and often played together.
- Young **Joseph** took care of the family's pigs in addition to doing odd jobs around the house.
- **Maurice** really was confused by the chaos caused by the explosion. By going back toward the house, he put himself and Alexis at great risk.
- **Buck Tavern** was the real meeting place for the family in case of emergency.
- **Sophie** and **Joseph** did go the wrong way and got lost in the woods on that terrible day.
- **Papa**'s full name was Eleuthère Irénée du Pont, but his family and friends called him Irénée. He started Eleutherian Mills in 1802. It was the first powder mill of its kind in America.
- **Irénée** built the family house close to the mills because he believed a boss should share the same risks as his workers.
- In 1816, **Irénée** built a school, called the Brandywine Manufacturers' Sunday School, that offered free education to the workers and their children.
- **Victorine**, **Tata**, and **Sophie** were among the first teachers at the Sunday School. Since children had to work six days a week, Sunday was the only day when they could attend school.
- **The Great Explosion** happened at 9:00 am on March 19, 1818. Thirty-four people died. It was heard over three miles away in Wilmington.
- As a result of the accident, **Irénée** arranged to help care for the widows and their children.

The Journey Begins...

In 1799, the du Pont family sailed from France to begin a new life in America. The voyage on the *American Eagle* was long and difficult. The ship leaked and the captain lost his way twice. By the end of the journey, the food had run out and the group had almost starved.

Upon arriving in the US, Irénée du Pont had to figure out how to support his family. In France, he had learned how to make quality black powder. He decided to build powder mills along the Brandywine River. The mills were built to be as safe as possible. But building was expensive and money quickly ran low.

Mr. du Pont worked long hours and often traveled for business. Although he worked hard, he made time for his family and his children adored him.

Eleuthère Irénée du Pont de Nemours (1771–1834)
Portrait by Rembrandt Peale, 1831, Oil on Canvas, Courtesy Private Collection.

Life in the house was filled with studies, chores, music, and visitors. Tata played the piano. Sophie loved to dance and draw cartoons. Alexis made everyone laugh. Important people visited on occasion. Even the President of the United States toured the mills in 1817.

Over time, Mama relied on Victorine to run the household and teach the children. Sophie's love of learning turned into a love of teaching. She took her first teaching job just before her fifteenth birthday. Henry went to college at West Point and then came back to run the mill with Alexis. Tata followed Victorine to become head of the Sunday School.

From the beginning, the dangers of the mills loomed in the background. Everyone knew that even the smallest spark could cause an explosion. At forty-one, Alexis would lose his life trying to prevent a blast.

In 1837, the grown children took control of the DuPont powder mills. Remarkable for the nineteenth century, the women joined in business meetings on equal terms with the men. The mills finally closed in 1921 when dynamite replaced black powder as a more powerful explosive that was easier to transport. The DuPont Company, however, continued to be successful by developing new products, like Nylon and Neoprene, as well as other materials that changed the way countless products were made.

Water Power and The Mills

In 1818, electricity was not yet available. Irénée du Pont built his mills so he could use the flow of the Brandywine River to power the machines. He created canals, called mill races, to guide water from the river toward water wheels. At the end of the mill race was a dam. The dam stopped the flow of the river into the canal.

When the mills needed power, the dam was opened and water rushed into the canals toward a water wheel. The force of the water made the wheel turn. The water wheel was connected to a giant gear. As the water wheel turned, so did the gear. That gear then turned the next gear in line, and so on. This process continued until the force from the river moved all the gears, generating enough power for the machines to grind, mix, or polish. The system worked very well.

Eleutherian Mill Rules

The powder mill was a very dangerous place to work. Only men worked inside the mills and there were many rules they had to follow. For instance, workers could not wear any metal. Even their shoes could not have metal nails in the heels. If metal scraped the stone floor or wall, it could cause a tiny spark. That spark would be enough to cause the powder to explode. Every day before work, the men were checked for matches and metal to prevent any accidents. Here are some of the other rules they had to follow. Mr. du Pont posted these rules for the mill in 1811:

The following rules shall be strictly observed by every one of the men employed in the factory:

- *They will keep the greatest regularity in works*
- *All kind of play or disorderly fun is prohibited*
- *No kind of spirituous liquors is allowed*
- *Any man who wants to absent himself must ask M. Dalmas or M. du Pont*
- *No strangers of any description are allowed admittance to the works or the yard of the powder mills*
- *The boats shall be locked at 7 o'cloke in winter and 9 o'cloke in summer. None shall be allowed to cross the creek after said hours.*

The Path of the Great Explosion

The process of making black powder in 1818 involved several steps: cleaning, mixing, and grinding ingredients; polishing the powder; and packing and storing barrels for shipment. Each step was dangerous and housed in a separate mill or building.

Mr. du Pont built his mills with safety in mind. Three walls were made of stone, two to three feet thick, and one wall was made of wood. In the event of an explosion, the wooden wall would blow outward sending the blast toward the river instead of toward other buildings or homes. In spite of the safety measures, flying sparks from a fire could jump from one building to the next on the wind. That's what happened on March 19, 1818. The Great Explosion was actually a series of explosions as one mill caught fire after another.

Dust Mill

- In the Dust Mill, also called the Glazing Mill, black powder was tumbled in glazing barrels until the edges were smooth or polished.
- The dust from this process was very flammable.
- It was thought that one of the machines set off a spark that started the explosions.

Pounding Mill

- In this building, also called the Stamp Mill, ingredients were ground and mixed together using mortar and pestle.
- Notice how this building is designed for safety. Can you see that three of the sides are made of stone and the fourth is wooden? This building also appears in the painting from 1806 in the front of this book. Can you find it?

Granary

- This building, also called the Graining Mill, was the third to explode.
- Here black powder was broken up and passed through a strainer to form small pieces.

Magazine

- Black powder was stored in this building before it was shipped.
- The magazine was the last building to explode.
- It held thirty-two tons of black powder on the day of the explosion. The blast was heard 3.5 miles away. Can you imagine? It would take you over an hour to walk that far!

How Black Powder Helped Build Our Nation

When the du Pont children were growing up, the United States was young and changing fast. In 1803, Thomas Jefferson bought 827,000 square miles of land stretching from Louisiana to Minnesota. The Louisiana Purchase almost doubled the size of the country and offered people a chance to create new lives.

DuPont Conestoga Powder Wagon Near Brandywine Mills. From the DuPont Company Powder Yards and Neighboring Communities Photographs (Acc. 2017.226), Box 9, Folder 6.

Suddenly, wagon trains of settlers began heading west. There were no towns, no roads, and no cleared land in the frontier. People hunted for food to eat and furs to keep them warm. Early American settlers depended on black powder to live.

Black powder was an important explosive. It was used for hunting, protection, clearing rocks and removing tree stumps from fields to prepare the way for planting and building. These tasks often meant the difference between life and death in the wilderness.

Travel in those days was slow. (It took over a week to go from Philadelphia to Boston!) People needed more and more roads. Many roads could not have been completed without black powder clearing the way.

In 1814, the first successful train locomotive was built. It introduced a new way to travel and carry goods. But there were no railways in America in the early nineteenth century. Black powder was needed to open the route for thousands of miles of railroad tracks.

As the country grew, people depended on coal for fuel and iron for machinery. The challenge was that coal and iron lay buried in the ground. Black powder was used to blast deep holes in the earth so miners could bring rocks and minerals to the surface.

Black powder played an important role in helping our country grow and survive. But it was also dangerous and could explode if not handled very carefully. By 1921, dynamite replaced it as a more powerful explosive. The DuPont Company then began creating other products, and over the years their many important inventions have continued to change and improve the way we live.

The DuPont Company used Conestoga wagons like this to transport black powder.

Why Portraits Were Important in the 1800s

Just like today, people in the nineteenth century liked to have pictures of themselves. But there were no cameras when Sophie, Tata, and Henry were children. The very first photograph was not taken until 1826. Then, for a long time, cameras were not very good for taking pictures of people. In the 1840s, a person would have to sit still for one full minute if they wanted to be photographed. That's why people rarely smiled in early photographs. Try holding a smile for a full minute. It's hard!

In the early 1800s a common way to record what people looked like was to have an artist paint their portrait. A portrait is a painting of a person often showing just their head and shoulders. The du Pont's had portraits painted of many of their family members. You can see some of their portraits in the back of this book.

Profiles of Eleuthera and Sophie in ink and watercolor, thought to have been done by Eleuthera du Pont around 1820.

The portraits of Victorine, Eleuthera (Tata), and Sophie were painted by the same artist, Rembrandt Peale. Mr. Peale lived in the Philadelphia area. He was famous for his portraits of Presidents George Washington and Thomas Jefferson. Without portraits, and art in general, we would have little idea of how people in those days looked or what they wore.

Glossary

Archive – a place where historical documents and papers are kept.

Bilingual – being able to speak two languages well.

Chronicle – a written description of a series of events.

Courage – the ability to do something that frightens you.

Eleutherian Mills – the name of the original mills owned by the du Pont family, which were known for producing black powder.

Foyer – entrance hall in a house or building.

Magazine – a warehouse; a place to store items.

Mes enfants – (French.) Translation: *My children.*

Mortar and pestle – a mortar is a type of bowl and a pestle is like a club. The pestle is used to crush ingredients in the mortar.

Nylon – a strong material used in some clothes, parachutes, and ropes, among other products.

Neoprene – artificial rubber often used in wet-suits, boots, and other products that can get wet.

Plaster – a coating for a wall or ceiling.

Sash – the part of the window that holds the glass in place.

Sand Hole – a place on the side of the hill at Eleutherian Mills where workers dug for soil to be used in the construction of powder mill buildings.

A Visit to Hagley Archives

Sophie and Tata wrote hundreds of letters throughout their lives. Here is a letter Sophie wrote when she was eleven to Victorine who was traveling at the time.

The rules for punctuation and spelling were different in 1821. In those days, people often used different spellings for the same word and sometimes left out punctuation.

February 29th 1821

My dear sister

I hope you did not stay all night in the packet as you had forgotten your cakes. Yesterday when you were gone we fixed the baby house and then went to scool I wrote while poly read in Human Manners. I sewed the remainder of the morning. Henry spent the afternoon at Lena's allthougth it raind. he read to us last night in Aunt Mary's tales for Girls. he is gone with mama to see Francis and has been very good. I am writing with a pen of Poly's mending for Mr Donner has not comme to yet to day though it is very late. I am in a hury for mama gave me leave to go and take a walk as she say's the change of air is good for the hooping caugh. I suppose you will go to see Mrs Hues to day as it is such fine weather. Poly desires me to remind you of the suspender cotton which you promised to bye. you must not say this letter is two short for I have made it as long as I could. I spent the greatest part of the night in caughing which is very disagreable. Lyly and Henry send their best love to you Good By dear Victorine and believe me ever your affectionate Sister

Sophia

francis est a peu près de même que dimanche

cheres filles, Je vous aime plus que je

Notice the different handwriting at the bottom of the page. That's where Mama wrote a message in French. Paper was expensive. People tried to use every inch of the paper whenever they could. They even used the edges!

Can you figure out what the letter says? Check the next page to see if you are right.

Tips for Saving Letters

Letters play an important role in teaching us about life at Eleutherian Mills. They are a great way to learn about people from other times and places. If you come across an old letter in your house, here are five tips to help you save it for years to come.

1. ***Wash your hands before you touch.***
   Wash your hands with soap and water. The oil and dirt on your skin can harm the letters.

2. ***Be gentle.***
   Handle old letters carefully. The paper may tear easily, especially if it has been folded or if it is old. Unfold the letter slowly.

3. ***Enjoy the story.***
   Some people say ordinary letters don't tell us much. That is not usually true. Letters about everyday things can tell us what life used to be like when they were written.

4. ***Save the envelope.***
   There are usually three important items that can be found on an envelope — a postmark, a stamp, and an address. The postmark tells us where the letter came from and when it was sent. The stamp lets us know how much it cost to send the letter, and the address tells us where the person receiving the letter lived, studied, or worked at the time.

5. ***Put the letter in a safe place.***
   We have du Pont family letters today because someone took care of them over the years. The best way to save a letter is to put the unfolded letter into a plastic folder or sleeve. Then store your letter in a box big enough that the letter doesn't bend. Through old letters you might learn a story you never knew before. Then you can write a book of your own.

What did Sophie Write to Victorine?

Here is a typed version of Sophie's letter. What did you learn about Sophie's day?

My dear sister February 27, 1821

I hope you did not stay all night in the packet* as you had forgotten your cakes. Yesterday when you were gone we fixed the baby house and then went to school. I wrote while Polly read in Human Manners. I sewed the remainder of the morning. Henry spent the afternoon at Lena's although it rained. He read to us last night in Aunt Mary's Tales for Girls. He is gone with Mama to see Francis and has been very good. I am writing with a pen of Polly's. Mending for Mr. Donner has not come yet today though it is very late. I am in a hurry for Mama gave me leave to go and take a walk as she says the change of air is good for the whooping cough. I suppose you will go to see Mrs. Hues today as it is such fine weather. Polly desires me to remind you of the suspender cotton which you promised to buy. You must not say this letter is too short for I have made it as long as I could. I spent the greatest part of the night in coughing which is very disagreeable. Lily and Henry send their best love to you. Goodbye dear Victorine and believe me ever your affectionate sister,

Sophia

*A packet is a type of boat

Learn More

Websites:

Hagley Museum and Library
https://www.hagley.org/
Learn more about Eleutherian Mills and Hagley. Plan a visit. See original art and letters created by Sophie and Tata and other family members in the Digital Archives.

Delaware Historical Society
http://dehistory.org/
Visit the site to find additional programs and materials for students.

Delaware Public Archives
https://archives.delaware.gov/
Find out about the many mills in Delaware history.

Library of Congress
https://www.loc.gov/collections/
Find numerous articles and images about the period in the Digital Collections.

Books for kids:

Domnauer, Teresa. *Westward Expansion (A True Book)*. New York: Children's Press, 2010.
Kirchner, Jason. *Delaware (States)*. Mankato: Capstone Press, 2016.
McDaniel, Melissa. *The Industrial Revolution (Cornerstones of Freedom: Third Series)*. New York: Children's Press, 2012.
Miller, Amy. *Delaware (From Sea to Shining Sea)*. New York: Children's Press, 2009.
Perritano, John. *The Transcontinental Railroad (A True Book)*. New York: Children's Press, 2010.

Bibliography

Barton, David, and Nigel Hall, eds. *Letter Writing as a Social Practice*, 1-41. Amsterdam: John Benjamins, 2000.

duPont, William Hulbert. *Explosions at the DuPont Powder Mills* [monograph], 1999.

Dutton, William. *DuPont One Hundred and Forty Years*. New York: Charles Scribner's Sons, 1942.

"Dreadful Explosion," *Democratic Press*, 21 March 1818, p. 2.

Low, Betty-Bright, and Jaqueline Hinsley. *Sophie duPont, A Young Lady in America*. New York: Harry Abrams, 1987.

Porter, Glenn. *The Workers' World at Hagley*. Hagley Museum and Library, 1992.

Smith (duPont), Eleuthera. Description of The Great Explosion, 1861-1873. Hagley Museum and Library Archives, Wilmington, DE.

Quimbly, Maureen. *Eleutherian Mills*. Wilmington: Hagley Museum and Library, 1999.

Meet the Historian

When you write about an event that really happened, you have to do a lot of research. If you are lucky, you will be able to examine primary sources like Sophie's letter. You certainly will read books and look at other secondary sources. If you are very lucky you will be able to learn directly from a historian.

Lucas Clawson is a historian who knows a great deal about the history of Hagley and the du Pont family. He is the person who identified and provided many of the primary sources that appear in this book. He is an expert on the history of the mills. Lucas spends much of his time researching interesting questions about the past and sharing stories about history with students of all ages. He often dresses in historical clothes and acts out roles of historical figures. Some day you might want to become a historian like him.

Acknowledgements

Special thanks to Lucas Clawson, Historian, Hagley Museum and Library, for generously sharing his boundless knowledge and answering an endless stream of questions about the history of Eleutherian Mills and the du Pont family. His expertise informed both the illustrations and the text. Thanks also to David Cole, Ph.D., former Executive Director of Hagley Museum and Library, for embracing the idea and arranging for the book to become a reality. Thank you to Jill MacKenzie, Executive Director of Hagley Museum and Library, for her support in seeing the book to completion. Thank you also to Sarah Snyder for her assistance in clarifying numerous historical details. Thanks to Jeff Durst, Bonnie Wirth, Tanya Looney, Dorothy Snyder, Adam Albright, Jennifer Johns, and Marje Kelly for their help in facilitating the research for this book. Thanks too to Carol Lemons, Maribeth Fischer, Cindy Hall, and the members of the Rehoboth Beach Writers' Guild for their enthusiastic support and helpful comments. Finally, many thanks to Jim and Nancy Holland for their outstanding editorial insights and their impeccable proof reading, Hillary Godwin for her excellent overall editing, and Jaqueline Cote for her creative expertise in designing the layout of the book.

Sketch of Eleutherian Mills by Eleuthera du Pont. From the Eleuthera (du Pont) Smith Papers, Winterthur Manuscripts, Group 6, Box 30.

Your Drawings and Notes

1775 Mama 1828
1792 Vic 1861
1806 Tata 1876
1810 Sophie 1888
1812 Henry 1889
1816 Alexis 1857
duPont

CPSIA information can be obtained
at www.ICGtesting.com
Printed in the USA
BVHW022242261120
594047BV00002B/2

* 9 7 8 0 5 7 8 7 6 6 5 7 7 *